AF417068

J.C. HULSEY BOOKS

THE WIDOW

J.C. HULSEY

For information contact: jchulsey1@att.net
Cover Art by Daniel Eskridge
Cover Design J.C. Hulsey
Published by J.C. Hulsey Books
September 2020
10 9 8 7 6 5 4 3 2 1

DEDICATION

To my wife of 59+ years.

May the next 59 be as great.

CHAPTER ONE

Lonely

As I stood in the front yard, the sun cast a multitude of colors across the prairie much like a picture an artist would paint. It was a glorious sight to behold, the works of our Lord. Fragrant cedar trees filled the air with that familiar pine smell. I heard a flock of birds fly overhead and looked past them at the puffy white clouds.

The hugeness of creation overwhelmed me as I gazed at the wonders of the vast sky. Yes, indeed I could watch sights like this for hours. I remember as a kid how much fun it was to sit for hours watching the clouds changed shapes. However, those days were long gone. I'm not a young girl anymore. I'm a grown married woman.

The summer sky grew bright as the sun peeked from behind a dark purple cloud.

I leaned my head back and looked again at the sky for the second time today. That was twice as much as I had looked at the sky in quite a few years. Those puffy white clouds I had admired earlier was gone and the sky was now a clear gray color. The bright yellow/orange sun was directly above as if watching my every move. It somehow made me uneasy. Why should I feel uneasy about the sun watching me? Perhaps it's not the sun that makes me so uneasy, maybe it's my own thoughts about Russ being so late coming back from town. But why should that make me feel uncomfortable? He's made many such trips in the past. Stop worrying, he'll be home before you know it. Yet, that niggling feeling stayed with me. Somehow, I knew this time, things were different. I couldn't put my finger on it, but I felt it deep in my gut that something bad was about to happen. I couldn't grasp what it was, but I had to admit something's going on.

Oh, how I miss his touch with those rough work calloused hands. Just thinking about them causes my body to shiver involuntarily. I think I know why I'm so nervous. It's the waiting. If only he would come home, everything would be alright.

I need to concentrate on the chores. Get settled into some sort of routine, then maybe my nervousness will go away.

How long has it been? I keep forgetting the date he left. I do know he should have returned by now. Maybe something happened to his horse. Maybe he decided to go visit one of his old girlfriends. If that's what you call a working girl? Maybe he got drunk and got thrown into jail. Hell-fire, most anything could be holding him up. Even if he is in jail or something, he could have sent word, couldn't he?

He knows how much I hate being here by myself. If we hadn't needed the money, he wouldn't have had to leave. This farm ain't making what we planned on. We're just barely scraping by. If that traveling man hadn't bought one of the hogs, we'd be in bad trouble and I mean most likely we'd have to pack up and leave this god forsaken place, but Russ says he ain't never leaving here. "This is my home." That's what he calls this one room shack. You have to give him credit though for doing all this on his own. Well, not exactly on his own. I been helping him right along. Worked blisters on my hands same as him. Why in the world would anybody want to raise hogs for a living is something I just can't wrap my brain around it. I will have to admit, when you sell one, it brings good money. Wonder where he's at?

It wouldn't be so bad if we had kids. It wouldn't be so dad-burned lonely. We planned on having at least four. Two boys and two girls, but the good Lord ain't seen fit to give us none and it ain't 'cause we ain't been trying. Sometimes plans don't always play out the way you want them to.

Also, maybe it wouldn't be so bad if I had a gun, but Russ took both the riffle which was out of ammunition and he took the pistol.

"Lot of good it did me to learn to shoot if I don't have a gun," I fussed. And I had become a crack shot hitting everything I aimed at.

"Don't be that way, besides," he said. "You should be safe here on the farm."

He climbed up onto the wagon seat, picked up the reins, slapped the horses' rump and he was off, headed for town. It took me a long time to realize that we wasn't in the pet hog business. We raised hogs to be sold to the butcher for money. How many times had Russ explained that to me? "That's what keeps going." *I sure hope that old wagon holds together for him to make it to town Something else we're gonna get when we sell enough hogs.'*

****

He did tell the truth in all our correspondence, but me being an easterner, I didn't understand everything. He told me about wanting to be a hog farmer. I had no idea what that was, so I told him it sounded exciting and it sounded like a very good idea. When I arrived here, at home as he called it, it was just a small one room ramshackle shack. Looked like it would fall down if you breathed on it. My first thought was, *'Hope the big bad wolf don't show up.'*

"We're gonna build a real house as soon as we sell our first patch of hogs." He told me. It seemed the hogs had better living arrangements than we did. But he did what he promised even if it did take a whole year. He built our real house all by himself with a little help from me. It's made of slabs of earth that he dug and cut into blocks, then stacked them on top of one another for the walls. He then cut some long tree limbs, stripped the extra limbs, then spread them on top and covered it with longer blocks of earth.

Okay. I reckon to you it might not sound like much of a house, but if you had seen the hard work and the love that he put into it, perhaps you would change your opinion. He also dug the well himself. Went down almost seventy feet. That took him about nine months of digging every evening after the sun went down. He said it was cooler then. Where was I when all this was going on, you may ask? I was right there beside him. I brought water to him. I cooked for him and let me tell you, that's a job in itself. He can put away more food than them blasted hogs. I ain't complaining, mind you. I didn't think I could love him when I first got here, but it didn't take long to realize he is the kindest, most considerate, loving person I have ever met and I have no doubt whatsoever that he cares deeply for me.

That's another reason I'm a little worried. He ain't never been this late before. Well, don't do no good to dwell on it. That don't get the work done. Dad gum it. That darn hog done slipped under the pen again. He sure don't like being penned up. Can't say I blame him much. I wouldn't like it either. I reckon I'll let him run a little 'fore I chase him back in there. The work sure piles up on you when there ain't but one of us doing it.

I reckon the cow is ready to be milked. Sure sounds like it. We was lucky to get two cows in a swap like we did. However, one of them died three days after we got her. I figure that salesman knew she wasn't gonna live long is the reason he swapped her to us. The one we got left is named Gertrude, but we call her Gurdy and she gives plenty of milk. Enough for us and the hogs.

Of course we got the garden, but we're gonna have to wait till next spring to plant again. Course the taters should be ready any day now. Fried taters sure sounds good to me. Listen to the way I'm talking. I would embarrass my mother and sister something fierce if they could hear me talk that way. I can almost see my mother's face and hear her scold me. I do miss them, but I figure she would be proud of the way I've learned so much about the farm and all. Yes, I made the right decision coming here to marry Russ. Like I said, I may have had some misgivings at first, but when he kissed me that first time, I knew right then and there that this was where I belonged. Of course he didn't kiss me right away.

He said, "We orta git to know each other afore we become man and wife in that way."

I think that's when I started to have feelings for him and then when we did kiss. That kiss curled my toes and made my heart pound faster than a locomotive.

He offered to buy my ticket back home if I wanted it, but after that toe curling kiss, there was no way I wanted to go back. You're probably thinking I was taking a big chance based on nothing more than a kiss, but it wasn't you he kissed. Of course I hadn't had very many kisses in my lifetime, but I had one now that was really indescribable.

When I gazed into his smoky eyes, I felt a magical sensation pulling me.

Love can be like a flash flood. Without warning it can grab you and drag you into its whirling depths.

Love although ain't as easy to get out of as the water. And maybe I enjoyed that feeling of being swept up into that wondrous depth of feelings called love.

****

Whoa, Gurdy, I'll get to you in just a minute. Just stand still. All that bawling ain't gonna make it go no faster. I think I'll make some butter out of this batch. I can give the scraps I been saving to the hogs and then when I get it churned, the hogs can have the buttermilk, after I have a glass for myself.

Turning from the bellowing cow, I headed to the little knoll behind the house. This was my special place where I would come when I was feeling sad and depressed the way I am now.

A soft breeze ruffled my hair. I pushed it back from my eyes and headed for the familiar place under the big Cottonwood tree. A place of solitude and comfort, however, today I didn't feel that comfort. What have I done for the calm feeling I always have in this place to desert me? Is it because I missed a few days coming up here? No. That can't be it, because I've missed days in the past and still felt that comfort. Perhaps it's my feeling of loneliness since Russ left. I've always felt that comforting feeling here. What is it now?

Oh well, if it's not here, then I need to go back to the house. Now there's a lonely place if there ever was one. Especially with Russ gone.

How long has he been gone? It was easy to count the days right after he left, but now the days all seem to blend together. He was only going to be gone for four days. Something's happened to him, I can feel it. He's laying in a ditch someplace. We only have the two horses for the wagon. We don't have an extra horse, so I can't even go looking for him. Now that's a bright idea. Where would I begin? It's fifteen miles to town and who's to say he followed the main trail. He could'a went through the pass or around by the old Miller line shack.

Walking back down the hill from my special place, it feels as if I accomplished nothing, absolutely nothing with this trip.

Might as well get to the chores. "I'm coming Gurdy," as she bellowed again and then again. "Hold on. I'm coming." Picking up the bucket just inside the barn door I sat on the stool resting my head against the cow's side. This wasn't one of my favorite chores, but it's got to be done like all the other things around here. As I said earlier, Mother would surely be proud of me.

"What was that!? Is it him!?" I jumped up from milking, dumping the half-filled bucket on the ground. Rushing out the barn door, I scanned the direction Russ would be coming, but didn't see nothing or nobody. I heard a noise in the house. I looked and sure enough the front door was open. I grabbed the pitchfork sitting beside the barn door and started toward the house. I was almost there when out came Butch, the boar hog. He rushed past me covered with something white.

"Oh no, you sorry slab of bacon, what have you done!?"

I leaned the pitchfork against the door and stepped inside. Butch had made an awful mess. Jars of vegetables broken and scattered all around. The white stuff that I had seen on him was from a busted sack of flour. Yes, he had made quite a mess.

I stepped back into the sunlight, "I'm gonna get you for this you ornery hog."

Of course, I knew I couldn't do anything to him because Russ said, "without Butch, we wouldn't have a hog farm," so I was gonna have to put up with him.

Going back inside, I began cleaning up the mess, then remembered I needed to finish with the milking. I'll get to this later. I thought I saw movement on the ridge, but then the sun blinded me, so I went into the barn to finish the milking.

CHAPTER TWO

Jeremiah Fist

Standing tall as he could at five four, Jeremiah Fist ran his hand through his raven black hair and looked down on the farm seated in the valley and said aloud, "Wonder where the man is? I'll stay here 'til morning, then if he don't show, I'll head on down there. That woman don't look too bad from this distance. But it really don't make no difference what she looks like. It's been a spell since I had any woman."

He stirred the coffee pot and poured the dark liquid into a tin cup. Holding it between his hands, he blew on it, then raised it to his mouth and sipped. "Umm," he muttered. "That hits the spot."

He continued to watch the woman as she hurried around the place apparently doing the chores. Fist thought back to the last time he did chores, he had just turned fourteen and had suffered his pa's wrath yet again.

That time he thought to himself, "I've had enough," and he picked up the pitchfork stabbing it into his pa's gut. He would never forget the look on his pa's face and the euphoric feeling that came over his body. He had felt that same feeling many more times through the years as he claimed the lives of others.

He spread his bed roll next to the fire and lay down, closing his eyes and pictured the woman from the farm.

The next morning came quickly with the warmth of the yellow sun sliding across his face. He sat up, looked around a bit, stood, stretched, then went a little way from camp to relieve himself. Coming back, he stirred the coals and added some wood to the fire. He shook the pot, finding it almost half full. He sat it closer to the flame, then dug some jerky and hardtack from his saddle bag. Standing, he turned and faced the farm below. He scanned the entire area and didn't spot the woman. "Did her man come back during the night while he was sleeping?" He said aloud.

He turned back to the fire, squatted, using his bandanna to grab the hot pot, he poured a cup of black liquid. Dipping a piece of hardtack in the coffee, and taking a bite, he chewed a couple times then swallowed. He finished the hardtack and coffee, then broke off a piece of jerky and put it in his mouth. Maybe the woman will have some vittles. Maybe some good home cooking? Now that might be almost as good as her. Fist downed the last of the cup, dumped the remaining coffee and grounds on the fire, kicked some dirt on it, saddled the bay and started loading all his gear. He glanced again at the farm and spotted the woman headed toward the barn. She sure looks fine from here. Bet she looks even better close up.

He slid his foot easily into the stir-up and pulled himself up into the saddle. Even after a good night's rest he was still feeling bone weary after the long ride from

South Texas. It was close for a little while, real close, but ain't no law dog smarter than Jeremiah Fist. He pulled the reins around and headed for what he assumed would be a pleasant visit. "Can't beat good vittles and a good-looking woman."

He stopped his horse at the edge of the barn, slid out of the saddle and waited for her to exit.

CHAPTER THREE

Stranger in the Yard

"Well, well, hello. You're good looking up close too," he exclaimed.

I stopped dead in my tracks and I knew he could see I had almost screamed. Quickly regaining my composure, I exclaimed, "You surprised me. How long you been standing there?" I asked, glancing around to see if he was alone. "If you're looking for a job, we ain't hiring," I told him, my eyes still searching the area. "This here's a hog farm and me and my husband can do everything that needs done. You can water your horse and then I reckon you better move on."

"I figured I might git somethin' to eat and maybe a cup of coffee," he said. "Ain't you gonna invite me in fer a meal or maybe a cup of coffee?" his voice sounded like gravel in a bucket.

"Sorry, stranger, but we barely got enough to get by. Ain't got none to spare. Get yourself a drink alongside your animal and head on down the road."

"Ain't none too neighborly, are you?" he snarled when he spoke. "Where's your man?" he asked, looking around. "He ain't here, is he?"

"He'll be back shortly," I answered hastily. "He's just gone to the neighbors to help them do a chore. He should be back any minute now."

"There ain't no neighbors close by. You think I'm stupid or something?" he rushed toward me.

I turned to run, but he caught my hair, don't know how he was so fast. He jerked me to the ground. The next thing I knew he was on top of me ripping my clothes. I struggled, but it was no use. He was a lot stronger than me. Eventually, I stopped struggling and let him have his way. When he was finished, he stood to pull up his pants, turning his back to me.

I struggled to my feet and started to run away, but he grabbed me again and snarled, "Let's go inside and you can fix me somethin' to eat."

He pushed me toward the house. I could hardly stand. Then I saw the pitchfork leaning by the door, it seemed to renew my strength. As we got close, I jerked my arm free and rushed to the house, grabbed the pitchfork, turned and lunged at him. He tried to get out of the way, but my movement surprised him and he wasn't fast enough. The pitchfork entered just below his rib-cage. I jerked it out and stabbed it again, this time a little higher.

His face contorted with a look of surprise, then to pain, as he fell backward pulling the weapon of death from his body. He uttered one last word and then his breathing stopped as blood gurgled from his lips.

I stood petrified at what I had done.

Why was I feeling as if I did something wrong?

He shouldn't have done what he did. I pulled my torn clothing together as best I could. His eyes were staring at me, sending cold chills up and down my spine, yet on second glance, I could see the light was gone from them and he was seeing nothing. I forced myself to stand up straight and headed for the house. Opening the door, I went inside, walked over to the bucket of water sitting on the cabinet. Grabbing a rag laying by the bucket, I dipped it in the water and proceeded to clean myself. When I was done, I walked across to the bed, stripped off my torn clothes and fell onto the bed. I lay there staring at the ceiling.

I could hardly believe what had just happened. And the thing that was worse than what he did to me, was what I did to him. I killed him. I killed a man. A living, breathing human being. A man was cast out into eternity by my hand. But he deserved to die after what he did. He was evil. He needed to be killed. But not by me, my inner voice continued to argue with me. *'Get a grip, young lady. It's been done. Ain't no undoing it. Get up, get dressed and go out there and bury your victim, before he starts stinking up the place.'*

I dressed in the only dress I had left. My wedding dress. At least that's what I called it. It's a much prettier dress than my work dress. Goodness, it's a little big. Have I really lost that much weight? It was a little tight when I got married in it. Better quit dawdling and do this. I walked past the dead man, barely glancing at him. I went inside the barn, located a shovel, walked to the back of the barn, picked out a spot and began digging. I dug the hole just deep enough to cover the body. Laying the shovel aside, I walked to the front of the barn, stopping where the body lay. I grabbed the man's feet and began dragging him to the shallow grave. He was so heavy I dropped his feet, went and got the wheelbarrow. It was a chore, but I finally got him in the wheelbarrow and pushed it to the shallow grave.

"There ain't no reason to bury his clothes with him." I began removing his clothing. First his gun belt, then his boots, pants and shirt. They seemed to be really good clothes except for the bullet hole. When he was down to his long johns, I rolled his body into the grave. I picked up the shovel and started filling it in. It didn't take long and when it was filled in, I stood contemplating what had happened again.

"What if I get pregnant? How do I explain to Russ what happened? Maybe I'm already pregnant, by Russ."

There ain't a whole lot I can do about it after the fact. I only hope God can forgive me for taking a man's life.

You need to quit dwelling on it. It's done and you can't undo it, besides if you was put in the predicament again, you'd do the same thing, now wouldn't you?

There is one thing about this that could be positive. You now have a weapon. Russ felt bad about leaving me here without a gun, but he said there wasn't any way he could travel to town without a weapon. "When we sell a batch of hogs, we're gonna get a bunch of stuff." That seemed to be his answer for everything.

I picked up the clothes I removed from the man, carried them inside and changed from my dress into them. They weren't a bad fit. I reckon it was because he wasn't a big man. The pants were a little loose, but I tightened the belt and saw they would be just what I needed to work around the place.

"I reckon I got myself a mighty fine horse in the deal too. Better put him in the barn."

I walked the horse to the barn and inside a stall. I removed the saddle and bridle then fed him a cup of oats.

"Now I reckon I better fix that hog pen. Sure can't have Buster running loose no longer. Russ would sure be mad if anything happened to his precious hog.

Maybe I can nail some extra boards around it so's he can't get out. Where did I leave that hammer?

Is that noon day sun a little hotter today than it's been? No. It ain't no hotter. It's because you're working a harder."

"That ain't a bad job if I do say so. Maybe a couple more boards on the back after Butch is back inside. Now all I gotta do is find that blasted hog and persuade him to get back in his pen. I sure hope he does, 'cause there ain't no way I can push or pull a four-hundred-pound slab of bacon. If he didn't spill the buttermilk, maybe I can use that to tempt him into the pen." I headed to the house to check about the buttermilk.

****

"Boy, I plumb forgot about this mess. As soon as I get Butch back in the pen, I'm gonna have to get busy in here and clean it up."

The buttermilk was right where it was supposed to be. Butch hadn't gotten to it mainly because he had made this mess before I finished the milking. What's happening to my mind? I picked up the crock of buttermilk and carried it to the hog pen dumping it in the trough.

I didn't see Butch anyplace. I'll go ahead and finish the repairs then I'll look for him. Gathering some more boards from behind the barn I proceeded to nail them in place.

I was just finishing with repairing the hog pen when I saw off in the distance, a buggy. "Now what?" I asked myself. "Who would be coming to visit? Or, maybe it's somebody coming to tell me Russ ain't coming back. Oh dear Lord, don't let it be that. Maybe I better play it safe and strap on my newly acquired pistol. Can't never tell, it could be more trouble. Where did I put that thing? Is it in the barn or the house? Wherever it is, you better hurry.

They're gonna be here any minute. I'm closer to the barn, so I'll look there. Did I leave it laying by the grave? Yep, there it is. I better learn to be more careful. I strapped it around my waist. It's a little loose, but I probably won't have to use it anyway. Let's go see who our visitors. Why, it's Roderick Garner, the store owner. How could I ever forget him? He told me he was going to marry me when I came here on the stage. I remember it well.

CHAPTER FOUR

Stagecoach Ride

Deep gray clouds blanketed the sky so the midday sun was almost blotted out causing it to seem like darkness had enveloped the land.

I clasped my hands in my lap as the stage coach jostled my blonde curls across my forehead.

The uneasiness I felt was like a ball of ice in the pit of my stomach. It was unlike any feeling I had in the past.

Was this feeling going to persist for the entire trip or would it ease as I drew closer to my destination? I shouldn't be apprehensive about going to meet my new husband. After all, we've been corresponding for months.

I feel as if I know him intimately, yet at the same time I feel as if I don't know him at all. Thus, this feeling that I'm enduring is probably just that, apprehension.

I glanced at the young man seated across from me and wondered about him. Where was he headed, I asked myself? He is very handsome. Those steel gray eyes and his raven black hair with that pencil thin mustache. What am I doing? I must not be thinking this way. My goodness, I'm on my way to get married. But I guess it wouldn't hurt to just look. After all I'm not married yet.

"What?" he was saying something to me. "I'm sorry, I was thinking of something."

"My name is Roderick Garner," his voice was so smooth and soothing. "I'm on my way to Alberton Texas to open a general store. May I ask your name and where you are going?"

"My name is Chloe Henderson," I told him. "And I'm going to Alberton also. Pardon my bluntness, but aren't you a little young to be a store owner?"

"I didn't know there was an age requirement," he seemed not in the least upset by my question. "I inherited a fair sum of money from my uncle and his wishes were for me to start my own business. There weren't any opportunities in the city, therefore, here I am on my way to Alberton. May I ask, do you have folks in Alberton?"

"No," I said. "I'm going to meet my husband there."

"Oh," his eyebrows raised. "How long have you been married?"

"Oh," I exclaimed. "I'm not married, not yet. I'm a mail order bride."

"Aren't you a little afraid marrying someone you don't know?"

"We've been corresponding for months and I feel I know him already. Are you married?" I asked, almost hoping his answer to be no.

"No," he smiled with amazingly pearl white teeth. "I'm not married. I haven't met the right girl yet, but I do want to get married, have a family, all that is very important to me."

"I do hope you find someone very soon," I said, feeling the heat rise to my face.

"I believe I've found that special one already."

"Oh, when did you meet her?"

"Only a few minutes ago," he said with a twinkle in eye.

"But I didn't see you talking to anyone. You don't mean . . . you can't be serious. I told you I'm going to be married as soon as I reach Alberton."

"But," he said emphatically. "You're not married yet. I think you and I would be perfect together. Now don't get upset, just continue sitting and visiting with me and you'll find you know more about me than your future husband. No. I won't call him that because, I'm your future husband."

"Don't be absurd, I'm moving to another seat."

"If you'll notice, there aren't any empty seats. We're on a stage coach and I'm afraid we're stuck together for the entire trip. Tell me more about yourself."

"I'm not talking to you."

"It's going to be a long boring trip that way."

*'What kind of idiot is in here with me?' I thought.
'He's got some nerve telling me he's my future husband.
Well, I'm not going to pay any attention to him.'*

The coach continued to bounce and sway with every bump in the dirt road and my stomach continued to clinch and un-clinch with every jostle.

'If only I had been able to eat some of that awful smelling concoction back at the station, but how could I if I couldn't get it past my nose?' Just at that moment, my stomach let out with an awful growl that caused my face to turn red with embracement.

"If I may?" he said as he reached into his haversack and withdrew an apple. "It sounds like you need this more than me. Please accept it without anything expected in return."

I glanced up at him, his smile was dazzling. "Thank you," I reached with a trembling hand and retrieved the apple. When my fingers grazed against his, I felt a sensation not unlike that feeling when you bumped your elbow. A sharp feeling seemed to travel from that touch all the way to the tips of my toes.

A little sound of surprise slipped from my lips when it happened. I immediately looked into his steel gray eyes and they looked to be changing colors as his left eyebrow raised and he smiled with those pearly white teeth an even bigger smile if that was possible.

I bit into the apple and the sweet juicy taste was enough to cause another sound to come from my lips.

"Hmm." I chewed, swallowed, then took another bite.

The sound of my chewing seemed to be echoing through the entire coach. However, this did not deter me from continuing to devour the apple.

Roderick Garner put his hand back into his haversack and pulled out a large piece of cheese followed by a handful of crackers.

"When you're finished with that fruit, I would be honored to share this little snack with you," he nodded and spread the small meal on a napkin on the seat next to him.

Taking the final bite of the apple, I reached and threw the core out the window.

"I can't begin to tell you how delicious that was," as I dabbed at my mouth with my handkerchief. "Thank you."

He sliced a piece of cheese with his pocket knife, placed it on a cracker and handed it to me.

"I shouldn't," I said, as my hand involuntarily reached to take the small offering. It was as if I had no control over my reactions.

"This is the way it should be," he said. "Two soon to be wedded people sharing a meal together." There was that dazzling smile again.

I was tempted to refuse, but felt my hand of its own volition take the cheese and cracker. However, my eyes told a different tale. If they had been daggers, Mr. Roderick Garner would have received a mortal wound.

But my upbringing had taught me to be polite when someone was nice, so I forced a smile through gritted teeth.

'Now, if I had something to drink, this would be perfect? This cracker is so dry.'

As if he read my mind, Mr. Garner reached into that magical bag and pulled out a bottle of wine, along with two small china cups. He removed the cap on the bottle and proceeded to pour the red liquid into those cups.

He replaced the lid, set the bottle aside, then reached for the cups, handing one of them to me. Just at that moment, the coach hit a bump causing the cup to spill onto my one and only dress.

"Oh my," I exclaimed, tears starting to blur my vision.

"Hold on there," he said. "There's no reason to cry. "I tell you what I'll do. I'll buy you a new dress as soon as we reach Albertson. How's that sound?"

That was all it took for the flood gates to open. The tears started to roll down my face and little sobs uttered from me. I wasn't crying about the ruined dress. I was crying because this Mr. Garner had been nothing but nice to me and that was something I wasn't used to. Of course, he had insisted that we were going to be married when I was on my way to marry someone else, but other than that he had treated me extremely nice.

"Here," he said, as he handed me a clean white handkerchief.

"Thank you," I sobbed as I took it, taking care not to repeat that feeling I got when my hand touched his before.

Dabbing at my eyes, I tried unsuccessfully to blow my nose quietly.

"Feeling better?" he asked, sounding sincere.

"Yes," I took a deep breath. "You've been very kind in spite of my horrendous attitude toward you. Would you be so kind as to accept my apology?"

"Really nothing for you to apologize for," he said, winking at me. "I must have surprised you with my declaration of love when we hardly know one another. However, I must say that you're on your way to marry a stranger whom you know absolutely nothing about when we already know more about each other in the short time we've been together."

"I know my future husband very well," I argued. "That is, as much as one can know about each other through corresponding with letters."

"That's what I'm saying," he continued. "I'm right here in the flesh and you don't have to accept a pig in a poke, so to speak. Do you even know what he looks like?"

"No. B . . . b … but I know all about him from his letters."

"Can you tell me the color of his eyes?"

"Well, we didn't discuss eye color, but he is thirty years old and is an even six feet tall. He owns a hog farm in Albertson."

"Sounds like a tough life. If we were married, you could help out in the store and have ladies over for parties. Nothing like the life on a hog farm."

"I don't know why you keep going on about us getting married. I told you I'm marrying Russell Kincaid and we're going to live on his farm. And we're going to be very happy."

"We'll see," he said with that twinkle in his eyes.

I settled back in the seat and closed my eyes trying to picture what the color of my future husband's eyes were going to be, but all I could see was Roderick Garner with those steel gray eyes, raven black hair with that pencil thin mustache and those pearly white teeth.

CHAPTER FIVE

Back On The Farm

"Who's that with him? Oh my, it's the doctor. Please dear Lord don't let it be Russ."

The buggy came to a stop just shy of where I was standing.

I glanced at Rodrick, then at the doctor. Both their faces were somber. I felt as if the air was sucked from my body and I collapsed to the ground unconscious.

I opened my eyes and looked into those slate blue eyes that I remembered from the stage ride.

"Just take it easy," he said calmly. "Doc is getting some water."

"Is it Russ?" I asked, trying to sit up. "Is he hurt . . . dead?" I began to tremble, I felt a coldness envelope me. My head was swimming.

"Here you go, "It was the doctor with a dipper of water.

"Drink this, it'll make you feel better."

I put the dipper to my lips and found I couldn't swallow. My throat was closed and all I could do was mumble.

"Is . .. s it . . . i. . . is it Russ? Is he dead?" I looked at Rodrick, then to the doctor.

The doctor took my hand as he knelt down. "I'm sorry, Mrs. Kincaid. Your husband is dead. He was shot in the back and left on the outskirts of town. I'm so sorry."

I tried to get up, but didn't have the strength. I felt paralyzed.

"Just lie still for a bit," said Rodrick. "When you're ready, I'll help you into the house. No, please lie still for a bit."

As much as I was hurting for my loss, there was a certain comfort lying there in Rodrick's arms. *'What's the matter with you, Chloe,'* I scolded myself. *'You just found out your husband is dead and you're enjoying another man holding you.'*

"I'd like to get up," as I pushed him away.

"Please, let me help you," he sounded as if he was begging.

"I don't need no help," I fussed. "I can do it by myself." I started to stand and almost fell back down, but Rodrick caught me.

"I think you should let me help, don't you?"

"Alright, but I still think I can do it."

He helped me into the house. "What happened here?" he asked surprised.

"Butch, that's our hog, got loose in here and made a mess as you can see. I was fixing to clean it up when ya'll showed up."

"Why don't you lie down for a little while?" the doctor said, as he came through the door.

"I ain't got time to lie down, there's work to be done. Always work to be done."

"As a doctor I recommend bed rest, at least until the shock wears off."

"Where is Russ?' I asked as I sat on the edge of the bed. "Why didn't you bring him home where he belongs?"

"We didn't find him for almost a week after he was killed. His body was . . . well we thought, that is, the sheriff and us, we buried him in the town cemetery."

"I want to bury him here on our place," I told them. "I think that's what he would have wanted too. Will you give me a ride back to town so's I can bring him back here?"

"Did you hear?" Rodrick asked. "He's already buried."

"Then, you'll have to unbury him!" I was shouting. "He needs to be buried here, on our place!"

"If that's what you want, sure we can give you a ride back to town." Roderick said. "How you gonna get the body back here?"

"Our wagon should be in town. That's how Russ took the hogs to market." I told them. "Oh, I don't know. I'll figure it out."

"We need to head back," the doctor commented. "It'll be dark by the time we get there."

"Are you going to wear that to town?" Roderick asked, pointing to my outfit and frowning at the gun around my waist.

"I'll change into my dress, if you gentlemen will excuse me." I stood and started unbuttoning my shirt.

Roderick and the doctor made a quick exit, closing the door behind them.

I washed off a little of the dirt and sweat and pulled my one and only dress on, then I strapped my new gun on. I took a look around the room, knowing I was still going to have to clean it when I returned. I opened the door and stepped outside.

The doctor and Roderick were already seated in the buggy. Roderick jumped down and offered his hand to help me in. I took it and God forgive me, but there was a certain tingle when our hands touched.

I settled in between the two men as Roderick climbed back in. I must admit I felt a certain comfort sitting between them, even though I think the comfort I felt was from sitting next to Roderick.

CHAPTER SIX

Reaching Town

It was dark when we reached town. Roderick stopped in front of the hotel. "You can get a room here until the morning."

"Take me to the cemetery," I told him. "I want to be near my husband."

"You really need to wait till morning," Roderick said.

"While you two figure out what you're going to do," said the doctor. "I'm going to my office. See you in the morning Mrs. Kincaid. Good night Rod." He started walking away.

"Please, Chloe?" Roderick seemed to be pleading. "Get a room and take care of matters in the morning."

"I can't go in the hotel," I mumbled.

"Why?" he asked. "You can get a nice soft bed. Your husband will still be there in the morning."

"I don't have no money," I was almost whispering, so Roderick had to lean in close to hear.

"You don't have any money, is that what you said?"

"Yes," I spoke a little louder. "I don't have no money. Okay!"

"Come on," he took my arm and led me toward the hotel entrance. "I'll pay for a room."

"I can't let you do that," I told him, pulling my arm from his.

"Don't be silly," he said. "We can call it a loan."

"Alright," I still hesitated. "As soon as I get the money for the hogs Russ brought to town, I'll pay you back."

"Sounds good, now come on," he took my arm again.

CHAPTER SEVEN

Hotel Stay

The clerk must have been bent down behind the counter because when he raised up and saw us, he was startled and began stammering.

"Who. . . what. . . oh, it's you, Mr. Garner. . . and a . . . young lady." His eyebrows shot up as if what he was thinking wasn't very nice. "You want a room?" the emphasis on the letter 'A'.

"Yes, Gilbert," he explained. "The young lady, Mrs. Kincaid wants a room and I will be paying for it."

Gilbert's mouth curled into a sort of smirk, "Yes sir, Mr. Garner. One room for the youn . . . Miss Kincaid, was it?"

"That's right," I spoke. "It's Mrs. Kincaid."

"Oh," Gilbert's face turned red and he said, "I'm mighty sorry 'bout your husband. He was a fine man."

"The key please," Roderick held out his hand.

"Oh. Sure," Gilbert handed a key to Roderick. "Room 4, top of the stairs, turn left."

Roderick took the key, turned and this time he offered his arm.

I put my hand in the crook of his arm and we started up the stairs. We turned left at the top and walked to room four. He handed me the key. I took it and unlocked the door, swinging it open. I stepped through and turned facing Roderick.

"I'll say goodnight," he said. "I'll come by and take you to breakfast if you like, then we'll go to the cemetery."

"That would be fine," I told him, recalling the time on the stage when he gave me food.

I sat on the edge of the bed and placed my face in my hands. I felt the tears start to pool in the corners of my eyes. *'What am I gonna do without Russ? I don't know if I'm gonna be able to take care of the farm by myself. Oh, I know I've been doing good while he's been gone, but I always figured he was gonna come back. I reckon it ain't doing no good worrying about it. I'll just take one day at a time.'*

CHAPTER EIGHT

The Cemetery

The sun was just making itself known through the tree branches, casting bright yellow streaks through the leaves.

There was a knock on the door. I had just finished dressing in my only dress thinking it really wasn't nice enough for a funeral, but I don't need to worry about appearances. I splashed a little water on my face, dried with the raggy towel, stood and strapped my gun around my waist. I walked across the room, opened the door, said good morning to Rodrick and stepped through. Walking down the stairs with him the thought kept nagging at me. *Maybe it ain't him. Maybe it ain't Russ. Maybe he'll show up at his own funeral. Maybe I'm going crazy.'*

"I really don't feel like eating, can we go straight to the cemetery?"

Of course. Anything you want."

****

As I stood looking at the grave, I was reminded of something my pa told me at his father's, my grandfather's funeral. *'The clothes and the body will rot away, but the name lives forever. I didn't understand at the time, but today I understood and I promised my husband's name will live on and mean something even though he's gone. I will work hard and make the hog farm one of the best in this county and beyond.'*

I felt all dried up. My throat was dry. I couldn't swallow. There was a tightness in my chest. I could hardly breathe. My face felt swollen from all my tears. I understood now what people meant when they said they had no more tears. I inhaled deeply and forced myself to be calm. I wanted to throw myself on top of the grave. I sobbed a dry moaning sound. Roderick offered his arm. At first, I pushed it away, but when he insisted, I placed my hand on it. He gently guided me away from my sweetheart, away from my one and only, my soulmate, my love, my life. *'How was I going to survive without my Russell?'*

"Let's take you back to the hotel," Roderick said. "I'll get the doctor to give you something to help you rest."

"I ain't got time to rest. I gotta git back and take care of the animals."

"Mr. Jenkins is taking care of everything until you can figure out what you're going to do with the place."

"What do you mean? What am I gonna do with the place? I'm going to run it and it's gonna be the best hog farm in three counties just like Russ and me planned."

"Chloe, you've got to be reasonable," he almost yelled.

"A woman alone can't run a hog farm."

"I been doing a fairly decent job when Russ went to town to sell hogs or to get supplies," I hoisted myself up to almost the same height as him.

"Yes," he continued. "You done a good job when you knew he was coming back. I'm sorry, but he ain't coming back this time. The work is gonna stack up on you so fast, before you know it the farm will be so rundown nobody will want to buy it."

"I reckon that'll be okay, 'cause I ain't gonna sell it. This farm was a dream of Russ and me and by golly that dream is gonna continue."

"That dream could become a nightmare before you even recognize it's happening."

"I appreciate your concern, but right now I got to check to see if Russ sold those hogs he brought to town, then locate our wagon and get back out yonder."

"If you got your mind made up, then at least let me walk with you to the butcher shop." He held out his arm and I placed my hand in the crook.

CHAPTER NINE

Missing Meat

The butcher shop was closed.

"That's odd," Roderick said, looking up and down the street. "I don't think Bert's been closed one day since I came to town."

"Let's check in back. Maybe he's doing something back there."

We stepped off the boardwalk and walked through the alley.

"There's our wagon," I nodded to the dilapidated wagon, empty, I might add.

"He's not here," Roderick glanced in every direction. "And the hog pens are empty."

"Try the door. Maybe he's in the back room."

He stepped up on the small porch and twisted the door knob. The door swung open.

"Come on," he motioned to me, as he stepped inside.

It was dark and damp and smelled like raw meat, just like you would expect from a butcher shop. We walked around the whole room looking behind every nook and cranny. Bert Honeycutt wasn't here. I walked to the door to the front part of the shop and opened it. He wasn't there either. However, there was one thing that was odd. There wasn't any meat in the shop anywhere.

"Where can he be?" Roderick asked.

"I think I'd like to know where the two hogs Russ brought to town are at."

"I think Bert missing is a lot more important than a couple of hogs."

"I know, but I need the money from selling them or I'm gonna be in big trouble."

"Let's go see the sheriff and tell him about Bert."

"Okay," I followed him back through the alley. We crossed the street and headed to the jail.

We were almost to the door when it opened and Sheriff Francis Bartholomew stepped out onto the boardwalk.

He looked up and said, "Well, howdy, Rod. Did you want to see me?" He looked at me and commented. "I'm mighty sorry for your loss, Mrs. Kincaid. Russ was a fine man. He's gonna be missed." He looked back at Roderick. "Let's step inside the office." He stepped aside and indicated I should enter first.

The office was small and cluttered. A large desk, two chairs, a file cabinet and a potbellied stove. There was a door in the center of the room which I assumed went to the cells.

The sheriff pulled out the chair in front of the desk, dusted it with his hat and said, "Please have a seat, ma'am."

I thanked him and sat down. He walked around behind the desk. "Sorry, Rod," glancing at Roderick, as he sat down. "Don't have another chair. What did you have on your mind?"

"Frank," Roderick began. "Have you seen or heard from Bert Honeycutt recently?"

"Didn't you hear, Bert is dead?"

"Dead!" the words rushed from my mouth without even knowing I was going to speak.

"Yes," the sheriff explained. "We found his body early this morning behind his shop."

"How did he die?" Roderick asked.

"According to Doc, he was stabbed in the chest with one of his knives."

"Do you know who did it?" I asked, exhaling loudly. I had been holding my breath without realizing it.

"No suspects yet," the sheriff said. "But I have a couple of ideas."

CHAPTER TEN

Unanswered Questions

"Did you see my husband come into town?" I asked the sheriff.

"No, ma'am. I didn't know he had been here until we found his body on the outskirts of town."

"Was our wagon with his body?"

"No ma'am," he exclaimed. "It sure weren't. I never even thought of that. That means somebody forced him out there or killed him in town and carried his body out there."

"When did you notice Bert missing?" Roderick asked.

"About midnight last night," he answered. "His brother woke me up telling me he was missing."

"So, it's feasible that the two men could have been killed by the same killer."

"Could very well be," said the sheriff. "Now the problem is, who? Mrs. Kincaid, did your husband have any enemies?"

No," I told him. "Most everybody liked Russ."

"You said most everybody. Was there anybody that didn't like him?"

Well, Thaddeus Crenshaw was always coming around wanting Russ to sell him our farm."

"When was the last time he came around?" asked the sheriff.

"I reckon it was the day before Russ headed to town. Russ was mighty mad and told Crenshaw he better not come around again if he knew what was good for him."

"Crenshaw said some pretty mean things and then rode off. Come to think about it, I do believe Crenshaw threatened to kill Russ."

"'Looks like we got a suspect," grinned the sheriff. "I'll round up a couple of men and ride out to his place."

"I'm going with you Sheriff," I spoke hastily, without even thinking.

"I don't think that's a good idea, ma'am," said the sheriff.

"Of course it's not a good idea," Roderick was speaking loudly. "A woman can't go when there might be shooting."

"I got my gun, in case you ain't noticed and besides, I'm pretty dang good with it. Russ taught me to shoot and ride. He said learning those two things might save my life someday." I stood tall and continued. "For you gentlemen's information, I done killed me a bad guy just recently. What do you think about that?"

"You saying you killed a man?" the sheriff questioned. "When. . . . where. . .? You just saying that so you can go on this little trip?"

"No," I said proudly. "A man came to the farm and had his way with me and afterwards I killed him. If you don't believe me, I can show you where he's buried.

"Okay," said the sheriff, letting out a big breath. "I'm gonna let you go with us, and when we git back, you and me is gonna have a little talk."

"Well," Roderick exclaimed. "If she's going, I'm going."

"You got a gun, Garner?" the sheriff asked, looking at Roderick in his suit he wore all the time."

"I own a store, Frank," Roderick told him. "I have all the guns you want."

"Just get one that you know how to use will be alright."

CHAPTER ELEVEN

Headin' Out

Roderick took off to get a gun from his store.

Sheriff Bartholomew turned to me and asked, "Do you have a horse, Mrs. Kincaid?"

"No," I replied. "Not here in town."

He shook his head and said, "Follow me." And headed out the door.

I hurried to keep up with his long stride. When we reached the livery stable, I followed him inside.

"Hank!" Bartholomew shouted. "Hank!" Dag nabbit, where can he be. Ain't never around when you need him."

"Is that him," I asked pointing to a pair of boots sticking out of a stall."

Bartholomew walked to the stall and shook his head. "Passed out cold. Come on, we'll help ourselves to a horse for you. Can you saddle a horse?"

"Of course I can saddle a horse," I grumbled. "Which one do I saddle?"

"Take the sorrel mare," he pointed to a gentle looking mare. "I've had her out before, and she was real easy riding. If you saddle her, I'll saddle my horse."

We were just stepping into the saddle when Roderick came rushing through the door wearing blue dungarees, a blue denim shirt and a pair of pearl handled Colt .45s strapped around his waist.

"Didn't know if you'd backed out or not," Bartholomew teased. "Them's some pretty fancy hardware. You know how to handle them?"

The sound echoed in the confined space of the stable as Roderick drew both weapons and proceeded to knock the horseshoes off the wall where they had been hanging.

"What's going on here!" Hank yowled.

"Nothing to worry about Hank. You can go back to sleep." The sheriff told him.

"What are you talking about. I don't sleep on the job," he said as he yawned. Where ya'll headed anyway?"

"We're headed out to Crenshaw's spread."

Rodrick holstered his six guns and said, "Was that shooting satisfactory Sheriff?"

"You'll do," replied the sheriff. "Now saddle up and let's move outta here."

Roderick saddled his mount and we spurred the horses and headed outta of town.

"How far is it to Crenshaw's place?" I asked.

"Couple hours," answered Bartholomew. "When we get there you two need to let me do the talking."

"I want to know if he's the one killed my husband!" I shouted, so's he could hear me above the noise of the horses' hooves.

We rode the rest of the way in silence.

CHAPTER TWELVE

The Shootout

Crenshaw's place came into vision just as the sun was disappearing behind the trees.

We had just reined up in front of the house when two shots rang out and the two men on each side of me slid from the saddle onto the hard packed earth.

I pulled my gun as I slid from the saddle on the opposite side of the house.

The horses had all stood still even with our bodies laying almost under their hooves.

Dirt sprayed against my boots as I ran for cover away from the house. I was lucky. I reached the barn and slipped inside.

My heart was racing ninety miles an hour and I was huffing and puffing like a locomotive.

I peeked around the door and noticed Roderick was crawling away from the horses. I needed to give him cover or whoever fired those shots might see him and fire again.

I cocked my revolver, took aim at the front door of the house. Lo and behold, a man holding a rifle stepped onto the porch. He raised his weapon and placed it against his shoulder. I squeezed the trigger exactly the way Russ had taught me, but not before he fired at Rodrick. The man dropped the rifle and slumped to the ground.

I holstered my gun and rushed to Roderick. He was lying on his back with his hand held against his side. Blood leaking between his fingers.

I knelt down and touched his hand. "You're hurt bad. Let me see if I can find something inside the house to help you."

"How's the sheriff?" he asked, coughing.

"He ain't moved since he fell off his horse."

"Maybe you better check, just in case," he coughed again. "Then you can look for something for me."

I stood, walked to the sheriff, knelt down and laid my hand oven his heart. Nothing, he was gone.

I looked at Roderick and shook my head, then stood and went inside.

There was a woman tied to a chair over in the corner of the room. Tears were running down her face into the bandana tied over her mouth. Her eyes wide with a frightened animal look.

I rushed over to her and said as calmly as I could. "You don't need to be scared. I'm gonna help you." I reached my hand out to untie her gag and she flinched as if I was going to hurt her. "It's okay, I won't hurt you." I said again. "Let me take this off your mouth." I reached again and she allowed me to remove it.

"Who are you?" the words bursting from her lips.

"My name is Chloe and I ain't gonna hurt you. Now lean forward so's I can untie you."

She leaned forward and I struggled to untie the knots. I finally got them loose and she jumped up and ran across the room. She grabbed a knife laying on the table. Holding it like she was ready for a fight, she shouted, with a slight Mexican accent, "Stay back, I'll kill you."

"I ain't gonna hurt you," I said as calmly as possible under the circumstances. "Crenshaw is dead. He ain't gonna hurt you either."

"Crenshaw is dead?" she asked glancing in all directions.

"Yes," I told her. "He's dead and there's a man outside that's injured. He needs help. Please put down the knife and help me find something to help him,"

She put the knife back on the table. "Come in the bedroom. There is things there for to help hurt man."

I followed her into the room where she walked to an armoire, opened it and brought out a small box. She handed it to me. I opened it and found bandages and some sort of medication in brown bottles.

"Thank you," I nodded to her. "Now could you boil some water?"

"Si, I will do that," she said in her broken English.

I carried the box out to Roderick. Kneeling down next to him, he opened his eyes and muttered, "What took you so long?" then he grinned.

"It's a long story, now try to relax while I look at your wound." I unbuttoned his blood-stained shirt. The blood had almost stopped.

"I need to turn you over to see if the bullet went all the way through," I told him as I gently pulled on his shoulder.

He tried to help, but the pain caused him to utter a loud moan.

I ain't no doctor, but it looks as if it went all the way through. I think if we clean it and put a bandage on it, you'll be okay until we can get you to a doctor."

I glanced up and saw the Mexican woman coming with a bucket.

"Here is hot water. Like you asked." She sat the bucket down. "This be your man?" she asked, looking at Roderick.

I hesitated. *'Was Roderick my man? Or did I leave my man at the cemetery?'*

Russ and I had talked a few times about what we should do if one of us died before the other. We had both agreed that we shouldn't be alone.

"Yes, he is my man," the tears began to fill my eyes. "Yes, he's my man."

The woman saw my tears and said, "You let me take care of your man. I do good job. Make him better for you."

I stood and stepped out of the way.

"My name Rosalita," as she knelt and began to wash the wound. "Crenshaw was my man, then he turned mean and beat me many times. When I try to leave, he tie me to chair. He not be like that all time. Only since he go to town two, three days. He come back and he mad. First time he hit me. I try to talk. Find out what wrong. He not answer. Only hit me. Then strange woman come. Fight with Crenshaw. Woman leave very mad. I think woman crazy in head."

I'm so sorry," I told her. "Maybe he was sick. Maybe something or someone made him that way."

"Maybe," she nodded. "He not be sick no more. I try remember the good days. Your man gonna be okay. Bullet go all way through. Bleeding stop. We need get him in house and into bed."

We carried Roderick into the house. "Through door on your right is the bedroom." I struggled with holding Roderick and turning the doorknob, but managed to get it open without dropping him

We managed to get him into bed. "Maybe you should go to town and get the doctor," Rosalita said. "I think he will be okay, but he should have a doctor look at it."

"I don't want to leave him here alone," I told her.

"He is not alone. I am here and I will take good care of him for you," she looked at me with the palest blue eyes I had ever seen. "We will be here when you return."

"Okay, I'll go," I told her. "But you better watch him and take care of him."

"I think that is what I said. Now go. The quicker you leave the quicker you get back."

"Alright. Thank you Rosalita."

"No," she said. "I thank you for saving me. I think maybe Crenshaw kill me if you and your man had not come here."

CHAPTER THIRTEEN

More Questions

The ride back to town was filled with questions that I didn't have the answers for. I wondered if I ever would. *'Why did Crenshaw shoot before we even dismounted? What was he afraid of? Did he kill Russ and Bert Honeycutt or was he afraid of something or someone else? Maybe the woman Rosalita mentioned'*

These thoughts wouldn't leave my mind as I rode into town. I rode down Main Street, turned onto Nelson Street, named for the doctor, and stopped in front of his house.

I slid from the saddle and rushed to the front door, which I immediately began pounding on.

After only a few minutes, which seemed an eternity, I heard his voice, "Alright. Okay, I'm coming. Take it easy."

The door opened and he was wearing his suit. "Mrs. Kincaid," he straightened his spectacles on his nose. "Are you alright? Are you feeling bad?"

"It's Roderick. I mean Mr. Garner," the words rushed from my mouth. "He's been shot. Please come with me."

"Let me get my bag," he turned and headed back in the house. Shouting over his shoulder, he said, "Do you need a drink of water?"

He returned shortly wearing his hat and carrying a satchel. "Your horse looks worn out," he nodded at my horse. "Perhaps you should ride with me in my buggy."

"Okay. Where is your buggy?" I asked.

"It's at the livery stable, which is where you can leave your animal. Hank should have my buggy ready to go when we get there."

"How will he know to get it ready?" I asked.

"We have a communication device of sorts rigged up," he explained. "There's a wire running from my house to the stable with a tin can on each end. Whenever I need the buggy, I shout into the tin can and he hears me and has everything ready when I get there."

I followed behind leading my horse. When we reached the stable the hostler had the doctor's buggy waiting out front.

"Thanks Hank," the doctor said as he climbed into the buggy. "Come on Mrs. Kincaid, get aboard and let's get going."

"I'll take care of your horse, ma'am," Hank said as he reached for the reins.

"Thanks," I told him, handing the reins to him, turned and climbed in beside the doctor.

He slapped the reins against the horse and we were off. "Now," he looked at me and asked. "Tell me what happened and where we're going."

"It's like I said," I explained. "We went to Crenshaw's place and Roderick got shot."

"Is that the whole story?" he inquired. "Or is there more?"

"Well," I continued. "The sheriff got shot too, but he won't be needing you to help him. He's dead."

"What did you and Rod get into?" he asked.

"It's a long story."

"That's okay. We got time."

I told the doctor the whole story, beginning with when we visited the sheriff's office and decided a visit to Crenshaw's place was necessary. He already knew about Bert Honeycutt being killed.

"Where is Crenshaw?" he asked.

"He's dead. I shot him."

"So, you're telling me three men got shot, two are dead, one wounded and you killed one of the men?"

"That's what happened and oh yeah, there's a Mexican woman there also. Her name is Rosalita."

"Sounds like you've had a busy time since I left you after the cemetery."

CHAPTER FOURTEEN

Missing Bodies

The sheriff's body wasn't laying where it was. In fact, it was gone. Did Rosalita move it? Crenshaw's body was also gone.

Jumping from the buggy I rushed through the front door and into the bedroom. The room was empty.

"Mrs. Kincaid," the doctor said as he came into the bedroom. "Where's our patient?"

"I don't know, but I plan to find out." I pushed past him and out into the yard. I hurried to the barn. There were no horses in the barn. *'What had happened while I was gone?'*

The doctor came into the barn. "Looks like nobody's here."

"Looks like you're right," I answered. "I'm gonna look around and see if I can spot any tracks. Maybe see which way they went."

"I think we should go back to town and enlist some men to help look for them."

"If we waste time going back to town, they could be completely out of the county by the time we get back. No, I'm gonna look now."

"It sounds like a good plan, but how are you going to look? On foot?"

"Yes, I'll walk. You drive the buggy. If we find which way they went, then we can both ride in the buggy."

It was impossible to search for tracks as the moon disappeared and black inky darkness quickly flooded the sky and left only the silvery stars scattered and winking at me and whomever might be watching.

"We may as well give up for now!" the doctor shouted. "It's only an hour or so till sunrise. Let's go back to the house and see about a cup of coffee."

"I reckon you're right," I answered. "Hold up and I'll ride back with you."

Nothing was said on the ride back. As soon as the buggy stopped, I jumped down, stopped turned back and said, "I'll brew a pot of coffee. You might wanna water your horse and put it in the barn. I'm tuckered out and think I might take a nap before we start in the morning."

"Sounds good," he answered. "I could use a bit of rest myself."

I opened the door and stepped inside. "How quickly things can change," I muttered to myself. I walked to the stove where a coffee pot was sitting. Picking it up I found there was coffee in it. Reaching over to the table I grabbed a cup and poured some of the dark liquid into it and took a small swallow. "Hmm. All I got to do is warm it up. Wonder if there's any biscuits or bread around here?"

The doctor opened the door and stuck his head inside, then came in. "I got everything straightened up out in the barn. You get some coffee brewed?"

"Warmed up what was already made. Looking for something to go with it. Ain't having much luck."

"Coffee's enough for me," he said as he yawned. "In fact, I think I'll pass on coffee and rest my eyes for a while. I'll go back to the barn."

"Ain't no need for that, Doc. You can have the bed; I'll stretch out by the fireplace."

"I'm gonna accept that offer 'cause I'm an old man. Goodnight to you." He stood and went through the door to the bedroom, pulling it closed behind him.

I poured another cup of coffee, drank it down as fast as I could with it being hot, then walked to the bedroom and knocked on the door.

"Yes, Mrs. Kincaid, what is it?"

"I need a blanket or a quilt for a pallet."

"Of course, just a second." The door opened and the doctor in his long johns handed me a quilt and a blanket.

"Goodnight again, Mrs. Kincaid." And closed the door.

CHAPTER FIFTEEN

Going Back to Town

The next morning came entirely too soon. I was hurting from laying on the hard floor in front of the fireplace, but I struggled to my feet in spite of my bones hurting. I heard a noise coming from the kitchen area and then I smelled it. Fresh brewed coffee. Oh, what a marvelous smell. It seemed to sink into my weary body and gave me strength to stand up straight and head toward that aroma.

"Morning, Mrs. Kincaid," the doctor turned slightly away from the stove where he was stirring eggs in a skillet. "I hope you like'em scrambled, 'cause that's the way you have to have them when they break."

"Scrambled is fine, but right now I need some of that delicious smelling coffee."

"Sure," he said, handing me a cup, then turned back to the skillet. "Eggs'll be ready in a jif. Grab a seat."

"Thanks," I said as I blew on the hot black liquid, then carefully sipped it. "Hmm." I murmured as it slid down my throat. "How long you been up, Doc?" I asked.

"Couple hours," he replied. "Don't sleep too good no more since I started getting older. That's something you don't have to worry about, I reckon. Did you sleep well?"

"Like a baby," I answered, then I remembered everything, and the weariness seemed to fall on me again. "I forgot for a minute everything that's happened."

"Time will heal all wounds," he said. "You just have to take it a day at a time. As soon as you're finished, we probably should head back to town."

"Okay," I wiped my plate with a piece of bread and emptied my cup. "That's was real good Doc. How come you know how to cook?"

"Living alone, you have to do a lot of things."

"You ever been married?" I asked as I stood and stretched.

"Nope," he smiled. "Never found a woman that wanted to put up with the life and the crazy hours of a doctor. You ready to go?"

"I'm ready as I'll ever be."

"I took the privilege of saddling your horse for you."

"I don't have a horse. I rode in the buggy with you remember?"

"Well, when I went to hook up the buggy there stood a chestnut mare, so I reckon you got a horse now. He' saddled and waiting right outside the door."

"Thanks," I told him, as I walked out the door. "This looks like a good horse as I slid my boot into the stirrup and pulled myself into the saddle. I pulled the reins around, gave a squeeze with my knees and headed in the direction of town. On the ride I had a lot to think about. *'What if Roderick is dead? Where could he be if he's still alive? What part does Rosalita have in this mystery?'*

"Hold up!" the doctor yelled.

I pulled up on the reins and waited for him to pull beside me.

"I was wondering who we talk to about all this, what with the sheriff being dead. He didn't have a deputy."

"Maybe the mayor can help," I said.

"I wouldn't count on Horace being much help. Ever since his wife died, he's been drinking away his sorrow. No, I wouldn't count on him."

"Well," I said, with a huff. "If we can't find no help, then I reckon we'll do what has to be done ourselves."

CHAPTER SIXTEEN

Decisions

It was still fairly early when we got to town.

"I've got an idea," I said as I stopped my horse outside the sheriff's office.

"What?" asked the doctor.

"If we can't get no help, I'll pin on a badge and deputize some men."

"You can't do that. The town will never stand for it."

"They'll have to stand for it or stand up for themselves. Besides they ain't gonna have no choice. If they don't join the posse, they'll go to jail."

"Maybe you might make a good lawman, uh excuse me. Lawwoman, at that."

"Who we talk to first?"

"Albert Finny, owner of the saloon. He used to be a decent man until he started drinking up all his profit."

"Let's go see this Mr. Finny. I'm in the mood to kick butt."

"I just hope he's sober enough to listen."

We walked from the sheriff's office to the saloon. It was awfully quiet for a saloon even if it was only mid-morning.

Doc pushed through the swinging doors with me right on his heels. The room was empty except for a balding man standing behind the bar nursing a bottle of rotgut. When he spotted us through his blood-shot eyes he perked up and said in a loud voice. "Welcome to the hottest spot this side of the Pecos. What can I serve you gentlemen?"

"Albert, it's me, Doctor Nelson. We," nodding at me, "want to talk to you about some serious stuff. Maybe you better get yourself some coffee so you can understand what we have to say."

"Are you trying to say I'm drunk? I ain't never been drunk my entire life," he slurred the words. "What do you have on your mind? Say, she's a girl. We don't usually have decent women in here."

"It's okay," Doc Nelson told him. "We got bigger problems than worrying about a female being in your establishment."

"Sounds serious Doc. What's going on." Albert stood up straight and if a person didn't know better, one might think he was cold sober.

"The sheriff's been killed and Roderick Garner's been kidnapped, and on top of that Mrs. Kincaid's husband was murdered."

"Yeah, I heard about Kincaid getting killed. Sorry for your loss, Ma'am. He looked at Doctor Nelson and asked, "What's all this got to do with me?"

I spoke up and said, "We need to form a posse. With the sheriff dead, we thought you might be able to persuade some men to join."

"Why me?" he asked perplexed. "I don't want to get involved in something where I might get killed, 'sides, there's plenty of other men that are more qualified than me."

"They may be more qualified with a pistol or a rifle, but you know everybody in town and they already look to you as a leader," Nelson told him.

"You really think they feel that way about me?" Albert asked.

"Absolutely," Nelson assured him.

"Well, maybe I could talk to some of the fellows and get them to join up." He puffed out his chest. "Who's gonna lead this posse? You said the sheriff is dead."

"If you or none of the men want to pin on the sheriff's badge, then I will," I told him.

"You can't do that, you're a woman."

"I'm a crack shot. I reckon I can outshoot most any man in this town. My husband taught me well. And I ain't afraid to use my gun when it's necessary."

"I don't know. I don't think there's a man in town that'll follow a woman."

"Why don't you ask them and let them decide?" Nelson said.

"I reckon I can do that, but I'm telling you . . ."

I interrupted him and said, "We're wasting time discussing this. If I have to, I'll go after them by myself."

"Alright," Albert said. "Come on."

We walked out of the saloon and headed up the street.

CHAPTER SEVENTEEN

The Posse

"Where we headed?" I asked.

"The Church."

"What are we going to the church for," I asked.

"It's Sunday. That's where all the people are this time of morning. I still don't know if this is a good idea."

"We won't know if we don't at least try," Nelson said.

Just as we reached the church, the door opened and the pastor stepped out followed by others.

"Hold on, Pastor, please," Albert said as he walked up. "If you could get the folks to wait, we've got some important business to talk to them about."

"Alright folks, please go back in and sit down. It seems Mr. Finny and these folks have something to say."

I heard a lot of murmuring and a little grumbling, but the folks did as they were asked.

The pastor walked to the front and motioned Albert to follow him. "Mr. Finny, please tell the folks what's so important."

"Well, folks, I think Mrs. Kincaid can explain it better than me. Mrs. Kincaid."

I stepped up beside Albert and behind the pulpit. "As some of you know my husband was killed recently. The sheriff, Mr. Garner and I tracked the killers to a house south of here. The sheriff was killed and Mr. Garner was injured. I came back to town for the doctor and when we got to the house Mr. Garner was missing. We, the doctor, Mr. Finney and I are here to ask you folks to join us to search for Mr. Garner."

"Why would we want to do that?" a fellow on the back pew piped up. "We don't owe nothing to your husband. He wasn't nothing but a bully."

"I'm sorry you feel that way. You may not have cared for my husband, but how about the sheriff and Mr. Harman?"

There was a lot of murmuring going on and finally Albert spoke. "I believe we owe it to the sheriff and Mr. Garner to help Mrs. Kincaid and the doc to at least try to locate Mr. Garner."

"Who's gonna lead this search party?" it was the man on the back pew again.

"Unless there's a volunteer, since Mrs. Kincaid knows the way, I recommend we follow her."

"I ain't following behind no woman. Woman's place is in the kitchen."

"What's your name, fellow?" I asked stepping from behind the pulpit.

"Frank Johnson," he said standing up to his full six foot four inches.

"You carry a gun, Mr. Johnson?" I asked as I stepped off the platform and walked down the aisle.

"'Course I wear a gun. Everybody does."

"I tell you what. I'll make a deal with you. Let's step outside and you and I will have a shooting match. If you win you can lead the group. If I win, you and everybody else will follow me, no questions asked. Deal?"

"Ha. Ha. Deal." He laughed as he turned and headed out the door.

Albert took charge like the leader Doc had told him he was. "You boys there, go behind the saloon and grab a dozen bottles and bring 'em back here."

The boys were back real soon and Albert told them to line the bottles up out beside the big Oak tree.

"Okay, when you're ready." The words were hardly out of Albert's mouth before Johnson had pulled his gun, fanning the hammer hitting four of the six bottles. "There you are ma-am," he said sarcastically. "See if you can beat that?' he slid his gun into his holster.

I slowly took my gun from the holster, slowly lifted it, took careful aim and squeezed the trigger the way Russ had taught me. The first bottle shattered. I did the same with the second bottle.

"That's okay," said Johnson. "She's just lucky, that's all. No way she's gonna hit anymore."

"Well Mr. Frank Johnson was wrong, because I shattered all six of those bottles. Then I removed the spent cartridges and replaced them with new ones. Russ always said don't never put an empty weapon back in your holster. You never know when you might need it and it won't do you no good empty.

I turned and faced the crowd. All you men go home, change into something a little more suitable for hunting kidnappers and killers. Grab your pistol and rifle and we'll meet at the jail in an hour."

Doc, Albert and me walked back to the jail where three men were waiting. One of the men was Frank Johnson.

"Good to see you held up your end of the bargain," I looked directly at Johnson. I then faced the other men. "You fellows don't own a gun?" I asked.

"Oh, we own guns. We just came to tell you we ain't going on your posse." With that said, they both turned and hurried down the street.

"Well, it looks like the posse numbers four. We need to go before that number becomes three," said a nervous Albert. I'm getting a funny feeling in my guts."

"Hang on a minute." I went inside the sheriff's office, rummaged around in the desk until I found what I was looking for. I grabbed four badges and went back outside.

I handed a badge to Doc then tossed the other to Albert. I pinned one to my shirt. "You still, willing to follow a woman?" As I handed the last badge to Frank Johnson.

"I made a deal with you and I'm an honorable man, so yes, I'm willing to follow a woman especially when she can shoot like you."

"Alright, this makes us official lawmen, so let's go catch these killers."

We walked to the livery stable where Hank had four horses saddled and ready to go. "I put enough supplies for three days in your packs."

"Thanks Hank. Sure you don't want to come with us?"

"I surely would if'n I could see more'n ten feet in front of me. Ya'll be careful out there."

"Which way we going?" asked Albert.

"I reckon Crenshaw's ranch is as good as any. That's the last place I saw Roddick, I mean Mr. Garner."

Albert led off with Doc following him and me and Johnson bringing up the rear.

"If I might ask, Mrs. Kincaid," Where'd you learn to shoot like that?"

"My husband taught me and I reckon I was a fast learner."

****

Crenshaw's place looked different in the daylight, but I guess with the body of the sheriff missing and also Rodrick's body, things were bond to look different. We stopped a few yards from the house and dismounted.

"Albert, you search behind the house. Doc, you search behind the barn. Johnson, you come with me. We're gonna head toward that tree-line." We hadn't gone far when we head Albert.

"Over here! I found something!"

Johnson and I headed toward him and saw him kneeling, looking down at the ground. "Looks like dried blood." I had seen blood and lots of it when Russ would butcher a hog. "Yeah, that's blood alright." I straightened up looking in all directions and then I saw what I was looking for. A body. *'Oh please don't let it be Rodrick.'* I begged silently. The closer I got I could see it wasn't him; it was a woman's body. I knelt down and turned the body over. It was Rosalita. Poor Rosalita. All she wanted was to live her life without any trouble. She had been so kind when she helped Rodrick.

Doc walked up behind me. "Who could and would do such a thing as this?" I asked with a lump in my throat.

I've lived a long life and I've seen all kinds of people. The way I see it, everybody's got both good and bad in 'em. It's just that some folks got a double dose of bad. I reckon those are the kind of folks we're dealing with today. Ain't much you can do to change that. We should get back on the trail. If Rod's hurt as bad as you said, then we need to get to him as fast as we can. Don't worry about Rosalita. She'll be here when we get back. We mounted and started through the trees and brush. "I guess I don't have to tell you to be extremely quiet."

We had ridden almost two hours when Doc stopped and pointed. Up ahead we could see a plume of smoke swirling toward the sky.

"Think that's them?" Asked Albert.

"Not gonna find out sitting here." I slid off my horse. Doc, Johnson and Albert did the same.

"Now what?" Albert asked.

"First thing is to be quiet. Doc you go around the left side of the building. Albert you go to the right." Johnson, you circle around and come in from the back."

"Which way you going?"

"As soon as you all get in position, I'm going in the front door."

I watched as my partners got into position and I stepped from behind the tree where I had been standing and headed for the door. That was probably the longest twenty yards I have ever crossed in my entire life. I stopped right at the door, leaned in and placed my ear against the rough wood. I could hear what sounded like voices, but I couldn't understand what they were saying. I thought I heard a woman's voice.

I opened the door as quietly as possible and peeked around the edge. I saw a woman, holding a gun, rushing back and forth from one end of the room to the other. She was flailing her hands around like a crazy person. I saw Rodrick laying on a cot in the corner. His eyes were closed. *'Please let him be alive,'* I whispered to the Lord.

Just then the crazy woman saw me and stopped so suddenly she almost fell, but caught herself. "Who are you!" she shouted as she raised her pistol.

"I wouldn't do that unless you're tired of living. Just ease it back down and live to see tomorrow."

I could almost see the gears turning in her head as she thought about what I had just said, then her hand slowly fell to her side, the gun falling to the floor as she released it. It was if she had given up, her troubles finally catching up with her and she realized it as she slumped into a chair.

"Okay Doc, come on in!" I shouted.

"Is that you Chloe?" Rodrick's voice was weak, but he was alive.

"It's me, Rodrick. Doc's here to make you better."

Doc rushed through the door, followed by Albert. Johnson didn't come in yet. Doc immediately went over to Roderick and began asking questions as he pushed and probed. "I'm fine Doc. Quit punching me."

"I will admit I'm a little surprised. I understood you were almost dead," he looked accusingly at me.

"It musta been Rosalita's doctoring. Now, let's get some answers from this lady. Let's start with you name."

She sat looking defeated and defenseless, and then she started talking. "My name is Shelia Hancock. Crenshaw was my partner. We were going to take over the slaughterhouse business in the county. He was going to furnish the cattle and hogs and I was going to run the butcher shop. However, Bert thought he could pull one over on me because I'm a woman, but I showed him."

"What about Russell Kincaid, why'd you kill him?"

"Just bad luck for him, he was in the wrong place at the wrong time. I didn't mean to kill him or anybody for that matter. It's this temper of mine. Something comes over me and I lose control."

"Why did you kill Bert?" Albert asked.

"He grabbed me when the gun went off and killed Kincaid. We struggled, I dropped the gun and grabbed a knife laying on a table. Somehow the knife wound up in his chest. I left him there hoping folks would think he committed suicide since it was his knife sticking out of his chest. Then me and Crenshaw had a violent argument and I left in a huff only to return after I heard all the shooting. I hid until you left to get the doctor. I then entered the house, stepping over Crenshaw's body, where Rosalita was making a pot of coffee. I hit Rosalita over the head knocking her unconscious. I stood surveying the situation wondering how I had gotten myself into such a mess, then I had an idea. "That's Rodrick Hanson, the store keeper. He's got to be worth a lot of money. I'll take him with me and figure everything out later."

She struggled to get Rodrick's unconscious body onto a horse. Once he was secured, Rosalita came out the front door unsteady as she walked. Shelia pulled her pistol and shot the woman. She then tied a rope around the woman's ankles and had the horse pull the dead body into the back yard a few yards from the house. "If I could go back and change things, I would."

"Why'd you kill Rosalita? She wasn't involved in any of this?"

"I thought she was gonna try to stop me from taking Garner."

"What's going to happen to me now? Am I going to hang?"

Doc spoke up and said, "I believe under the circumstances you will probably spend some time in a sanitarium where you'll be able to get some help."

I went over to Roderick who was sitting up on the cot leaning against the wall. "I sure am glad to see you." He said as he took my hand and pulled me down to sit beside him.

"Oh Rodrick, I'm so glad you're alive. I thought you were gone forever."

"Not a chance. You and I have a full life ahead of us. That is if it's not too soon after Russ' death."

"I know it's only been a few days, but it feels like an eternity has gone by. So, no, it's not too soon."

"Do you remember what I said to you on the stage coach all those years ago?"

"Yes, I remember very well. You said that you and I were going to be married."

"I'm sorry it had to be this way, but I'm not sorry that you're finally where you belong."

EPILOGUE

When Doc Nelson told the judge about Shelia's condition, she was sent to the sanitarium just like Doc suggested.

Frank Johnson was elected the town's new sheriff. Albert Finny sold his saloon and bought the butcher shop from the bank. "If somebody's willing to kill to get in the meat business, there's got to be money to be made."

Roderick sold the store to a newcomer that had arrived in town looking to invest in a business, then he moved to the farm with me. After we were married of course. He said he only wanted to make me happy and if he had to be a hog farmer, then that's what he would do.

We never did find out what happened to the hogs Russ had brought to town to sell, however the town council felt that since I was instrumental in bringing in the killer, they decided to offer a reward, which by the way, I accepted. It was just enough to carry me over until another batch of hogs would be ready for market.

Roderick and I have a little boy who looks a lot like Russ, however he is small in stature. The main thing that I think about is no matter what happened in the past, Roderick is little Russell's daddy.

By the way, we did get Butch back in his pen and he hasn't got out since.

Books by J.C. Hulsey

Angel Falls, Texas

Velvet Sky, Arizona

Angry Orchard, Colorado

Clear Stone, Wyoming

Itching Tree, Idaho

Windy Butte, New Mexico

Devil's Dance, Dakota Territory

Redemption Road

Red Rose

Rebecca

The Concho Kid

Ugly Mugly

GUTSHOT

The Last Ride

The Old Man

The Pistol Preacher

Shortland

Dynamite

The Concho Kid

Dead Man's Gun

Does Nora Know

Doke Walker

Brothers

Satan's Refuge

Shadrack

The Brute

The Decision

The Greenhorn

The Gunfight

The Hangman

The Old Timer

Trudy

The Waterhole

Welcome to Texas Hell

Some Stuff I Wrote

Some More Stuff I Wrote

Even More Stuff I Wrote

Newest Stuff I Wrote

Brand New Stuff I Wrote

Brand Spanking New Stuff I Wrote

Look What I Found

Oldest Coon Hunter in Somervell Co

(Compiled by)

Confessions of a Battered Wife

(Compiled by)